Constellation

SUNDIAL HOUSE

Constellation

Latin American Voices in Translation

Edited by

Elvira Blanco

SUNDIAL HOUSE   NEW YORK   •   PHILADELPHIA

**SUNDIAL
HOUSE**
New York ✦ Philadelphia

Book design: Lisa Hamm
Cover image: Victoria Colón Rodríguez
Proofreader: Liam Sebastián Ferguson

ISBN: 979-8-9879264-75

Contents

A Storm

Dialogues

Mere Diary

Smoke Shrouds the Earth

The Coming Desert

The Girl from Mexico

Constellation

A Storm

AN EXCERPT FROM *UN TEMPORAL*
(EDITORIAL ENTROPÍA, 2021) BY ANSILTA GRIZAS

TRANSLATED BY JENNY BURTON

IN ANTARCTICA I visited a black island, so black, on the outer rim of an archipelago. Our group was there for several days, staying on a naval base. From a distance, the island looks normal, but in reality, it's a ring of black earth surrounding a flooded caldera. It seems that thousands of years ago a volcanic eruption left it that way, with a sea-flooded hole in the middle known today as Port Foster. To enter the caldera, you have to pass through a narrow strait of imposing, majestic dark rocks; the sea strikes and clings to them all day long, smoothing them. Neptune's Bellows. What an astral and cosmic name to welcome you to Deception Island.

Beneath that bay, beneath the icy Antarctic waters, there's a volcano that's still active. So, there, on that island, two opposing extremes coexist: ice and lava, concentrated in an area of only twenty-five square miles.

The night we arrived we were told that if the volcano erupted, we'd only have twelve minutes to run, climb the mountain to the highest point, and descend to the sea on the other side of the hill where the penguin colony is—and where, best case scenario, we'd be rescued.

During the last eruption in 1968, they sent a radio message that said, "all at once, a shower of rocks is coming down over the bay and the beaches of Deception Island." A downpour of hot stones, molten igneous rock, lava, and ashes. Nature really roaring. Apparently, an explosive mushroom of more than three thousand feet rose, destroying everything it could find, and in that mushroom, there were lightning and stones exploding in the sky, and the earth moved, rippling and rumbling like the growls of a beast. A rain of fine, sticky ash fell and stuck to the ice and the soft December snow. Then it was night and then it was day and the eruption raged on and naturally not a seagull, cormorant, nor penguin, nothing, not even a bug, was around. "The bugs are wise; they knew long before I did," said a radio operator from the Argentine base who survived. He also said that the cloud seen from the bay was a "beautiful spectacle," and he was sorry a kitten and a dog were left behind at the abandoned base.

Today the island is all black, murky, with vapors hovering above the water's edge, hot white vapors called fumaroles which have a strong sulfurous odor. But underneath that black, carbonaceous rock hides the runnel filled with flowing lava. You only need to dig a little and there it is, enduring. Nature and its power. That power that surpasses you, leaving you small and insignificant, trampling you. The ice is there, a perpetual thin layer above the fire, coexisting in that tension, that fragile balance. Until one day the fire triumphs over the ice, and a rain of ash and bits of rock warn you that it's time to run. Then one will win. But for now, they exist there, together.

Apparently, the name of the island was a misnomer: they translated "deception" in English to *decepción* in Spanish (which actually means "disappointment") instead of *engaño*, as it should be. I still think both are wrong. The island doesn't trick or deceive you, nor does it give you something you didn't want. It's the concentration of all the states of nature, together, in perfect harmony.

We had a phone call recently where you asked me, terrified, how I was doing, who'd hurt me, if I was all right, all of this with an urgency I didn't understand, and I hurriedly tried to reassure you with no success. Not two minutes later you were telling me that you were waiting to see me at noon for lunch, it was chicken cutlets today. I said yes, I was ready, but I was six hundred miles away.

I told you about your new grandson, who, like a very small animal, is glued to my boob all day long. Smugly, you said he sounded just like me when I was a newborn. You could recall things from thirty years ago, but you couldn't remember how far apart we lived.

It was always hard for us to be away from one another. Over the past nearly seven years I've lived here, I've never not wanted to spend a Sunday with you. I'll never rid myself of the guilt I hold for not being there.

The transition to this place wasn't kind. The city always felt so fast and unfriendly. There were so many unknowns. The only thing I did know was that I had to get out of there. I was depleted from so much desert. In a bleak sense, the noise of this city held me. And although there were days when I missed the kind of sanctuary one has in their own home, I no longer had anywhere like that to return to. My house in San Juan had been packed up and rented out, and any idea of home, with my things and smells, didn't exist anywhere anymore. Nor did my mother's house have that aura of embrace and security that a parent's house is supposed to have: the foods you like, the single bed perfect for afternoon naps, the soft sheets that remind you of childhood, and that ease of moving through spaces as if they were your own. Since you left, your houses never had anything that would've belonged to me. I guess that was because this space you'd built for yourself only ever functioned as a place to visit. There's a song that goes, *por más que me mude de pueblo en pueblo*, no matter how much I move from town to town, *pienso que mi casa va a ser la misma*, I think my home will stay my own. Well, I didn't have that.

I remember details from the houses we lived in growing up, very specific things. I remember the apartment in Canada with the shag carpet and that huge park across the street, or maybe it just seemed huge when I was five. I also remember you with a cardboard box on your head like a television set, talking like Big Bird from Sesame Street.

I remember the house on San Luis Street, and the red and white checkered curtains on the kitchen window, and your desk full of rulers of all shapes and sizes and pencils that I always liked to play with. I remember your first desk in the attic at the Vesta house, and the picture of the windmills next to the dining room table, and the old radio always tuned to the national public radio station. I also recall the time when the power was out in the whole city and there in the attic, with that same radio we somehow connected to a radio station in France. Your workspaces in each house we lived in are always present in my memories, those sacred places where we weren't allowed to disturb you, but sometimes we were allowed to draw or play quietly with a friend.

There are those who say that building a home of your own is to seek to create a warm space where we're able to abandon ourselves indefinitely, not only to live but also to die. I like it when F. comes and says it smells like home, like homemade food and washed clothes and children, and us. Over the years, finally, I created that space for myself and my family, not in anyone else's house, but in a space of my own, here, the only place I want to be.

* * *

I dreamt recently that an anteater was nuzzling my neck, there in that flat spot under my chin. It wasn't scratchy or rough, but it felt a bit damp, like the nose of a healthy dog. Shiny. It was small but still reached my height of five foot six inches, and somehow it didn't scare me, nor did it feel strange.

I woke up. I nursed the baby, still so small and nursing every two hours. I thought about the anteater. I don't know if I'd ever seen one before, at a zoo maybe, but I couldn't reconstruct its physiognomy in my head. In the early morning, in that kind of limbo between sleep and watching and holding the baby close, I think a lot of strange things. I'm sure it's the combination of hormones and lack of sleep. In fact, I'm not sure if I dreamed about the animal or if I thought about it after reading something about anteaters on the internet.

I also think about what I'm writing. I dictate passages in my head that I'll later forget, or that, the next day, with a bit more lucidity, don't make sense and get deleted.

I think about how to finish writing this, how far to go. I don't want this to end up being a book about me. I want it to be about us. About me being your daughter, and the relationship that, all at the same time, binds us together and brings with it the pain of seeing you like this now. But also brings love, and all that you knew how to give me as my dad. And also about acceptance and letting go. About running away from that place, moving, pushing forward. Going along with the current and not looking back, linking arms with those alongside you. Having you now be my beacon, holding me close during that shot in the arm, the embrace of the night-time storm, the bedtime story. For my own children, being their support and their shelter.

I don't want this book to be a mourning, a suffering, a cry, a book about what it produces in me to see you transformed into that other kind of you, an amorphous animal, that, from a distance, glimpses what you used to be in the midst of all the strangeness that now consumes you. The animal disease that tore you away from me.

I want this to be a book that says that we were. You, my dad, Ansilta, your daughter, now mother.

* * *

When he couldn't fall asleep last night, my son told me he was going to wait until "the sky comes out" to close his eyes. He said he doesn't like when it's dark like that, he's afraid. I thought about that utterance and the innocence of being three years old. I also thought about the magnitude of things for him, which is not the same magnitude for me. I thought about how sometimes I feel like the ceiling is falling down on me in slow motion. I'm sure I'm missing something, I tell myself when I stand next to him and we lean our heads together, while I sing him the song that calms him down. Sometimes I'm in a hurry, you know? I keep moving appointments earlier, and when they ask me how old I am I always add a year, and when they ask me how old my children are I round up. It seems like I'm trying to get somewhere. But I don't really know where, or what for. I've always been a bit anxious. But now it's like I want to grow up faster, to get away from it.

As if moving forward in time could give me immunity from pain.

* * *

This photo is my proof.

It's my proof that we did exist.

It's how I know that on that afternoon in 1994 at my seventh birthday party, you were there with me. In the photo, you're holding me while my hands clutch yours. The balloons, orange, sea green, white, pink, and yellow, matched the decorations on the cake my grandmother had made for the occasion.

This photo is proof that we did exist, that those little hands holding onto you are mine, and that my expression, and yours, and that love, existed too, just like you see it there. Simultaneously normal and supreme. You held me while I held onto your hands. This photo, an expression of the relationship we knew how to have.

* * *

Today I was reminded of a very vivid image that resides in my mind, as vivid as it is horrific. I was in the desert and there, I watched how a snake ate a giant lizard. Re-watching the scene of a body inside of another body, half alive but still alive, wriggling its tail, but dying all the while, devoured by another stronger, more adept creature.

When the snake noticed our gaze, it kept very still, and in two seconds, poof, the lizard was gone. By now, it's a single animal coiling itself around some stick while finishing grinding the bones.

The shape of the other was still visible within its serpentine form.

I find it hard to see you, to look at you. I look away. I erase the pictures they send me of you. You're you, but you're also a stranger. Your stiffness, your skin, not yours. You're all of you, but not you at all, an imposter, a distortion, a withering. There you are, visible under all that skin that's not yours, just before the other stops writhing and finishes you off.

All the while I watch my kids grow up, things move forward. Buds emerge. It's a spring.

I tend to dwell on the subtleties of newborn babies. The little divots on their faces, their perfectly formed ears, their chubby, wrinkled fingers and toes, and the creases where their hands meet their arms, barely wrists. The blond fuzz on their backs. Their little teeth like pearls. They are the alive part. The other end of the spiral of this whole continuous circuit that's nothing more than nature: the form and the formless, what's luminous and what's already almost completely dark.

It's been diminishing for so long that the memory of the luminous fades and warps under the weight. Because you're there in that exact moment, a body half-devoured by that other. You're neither one thing nor the other. A thing that doesn't progress nor does it reach its demise, and merely sustains, there, in that formlessness of what isn't, of what doesn't resemble life.

* * *

I passed by a house that had a whole garden full of daisies in bloom and I paused.

It's December. Christmas is two days away. You always wanted to have those beautiful daisies on the table for Christmas Eve dinner. You wrote about it.

The bulbs are planted in August and with the heat they bloom, you explained, that time we planted them together.

You have to be sure there's ample space between them so there is plenty of fresh air around each one later on.

Daisies are lovely and wild. The latter most of all. In the popular unconscious they might be fairytale flowers, but the truth is they're quite untamed and free.

I like that.

My son brings you up all the time. He talks about your house, about taking a plane to go to your house, about the piano you have there. He lists his grandparents and names you. You are in his games and stories; you are part of his reality and his fantasies.

They told me that you cried when you talked to him and when he sang "Happy Birthday." He also told you that he went to watch the planes take off and that his new brother cries a lot. These days we all cry a lot.

✳ ✳ ✳

It guts me to think about everything that is backing away, going in reverse, retreating, about the tide going in and leaving everything exposed. Fungus, garbage, dead animals. To think we had such sunny and luminous times and then rewound the film, further and further back and there was no sea left to dilute all the filth, because the filth was always there. And now nothing would be able to save it.

It terrifies me to think about how this can happen to my family, even to the new one I've built for myself. That regression, the deterioration.

I once read that grieving the loss of a loved one is a place we don't know until we're there.

I think about this, and about the place I'm inhabiting with respect to loss in general, and to yours specifically. How it is and it isn't at the same time. How it will be, but it isn't yet. How it's there latent, how we know at some point it will happen and how, in the end, in some way, it already has. I think of you, papá, as I write this, knowing you're still there, but also knowing I can't read it to you because you wouldn't be able to understand. So, are you really there, and in what sense, and is it not a loss, too, that it's latent there, lacking only the final blow, the writhing snake? And now I can't help but wonder what that day will be like for me, when we reach that definitive place, on the other side of the bay.

I haven't seen you in a year.

The last time I saw you was a year ago in the nursing home.

You cried because you knew it would be a long time before we saw each other again. I cried because I didn't know if it was going to be the last time.

I never know if it will be the last, just as I never know if that phone call is the one telling us the unmentionable is coming.

Before, thinking about it used to make my blood run cold.

We talked a few times this year, I think I can count them on one hand. Sometimes you were there, sometimes you weren't, and it frustrated me.

Yet, all the time, you are here with me, with us. I think about the things I'd tell you about. About the kids and how they're growing up, and the new house. I'm sure you would've said it's very Buenos Aires, the way you like it.

I engage in conversations with the you you once were, not with the you there in that chair, in a solitude that is completely inaccessible to me.

I find it hard to talk about you these days. I realize I don't know whether to refer to you in the past or present tense. "My dad is an architect," and then I correct myself: "was." I feel others' discomfort, and so I avoid it.

Recently I was asked if I would rather you were dead, to spare you the pain. I froze; no one had ever framed the question to me in that way. I'd never verbalized it aloud to another person before. It hurts to write it.

There are people to whom words come easier. They're able to put their ideas and feelings in order. For me, the words get stuck, lodged here, trapped. They manifest in many forms: a lump in my throat, eczema on my skin, bitten fingernails, new gray hairs, a deep wrinkle between my brows, the anguish and the fury and the crying for the most unexpected reason. I think writing this is a way to escape. I'm able to talk to you as if everything were different. To lighten the load. You would always say, "in the end we leave with the clothes on our backs." Writing is also a way of leaving a trail behind in time. To write is to leave a trace. Words hurt, reverberate, heal, console, leave a mark, endure.

My grandfather also had a diary that was half planner, in which he wrote what he had to do in pen, and what he had completed in red pencil. I remember the last time I visited him, he'd written the date of my arrival and next to it: "Ansilta arrives, buy Coca-Cola." I always think back on that note as a gesture of love.

* * *

I made it back. It's been many years since I left.

I forgot the streets and the names of the neighbors. I only remember what it was like before. Now it's so mystifying I hardly recognize myself here, in this city where I lived most of my life. I feel like an outsider every time I come back to visit.

Here I linger with nostalgia. I associate everything with what it was: the houses that are no longer there, the streets that are no longer there, the family that is no longer there, the old man that died, the ivy that dried up, and the girl that wasn't, at least not anymore. In this park on that bench, I had my first kiss. On this street, along this route, I rode my bicycle every afternoon on my way home from school.

Here, in this city, you aren't here anymore.

Here everything seems extinct, muddy, brown, cracked, broken, dry. The paint is fading on the walls of my mother's house, and there are cracks where dirt gets in when the wind blows. Yet the pepper trees in the backyard grow endlessly and bear jangling red fruit. The dogs get lost and swell up and die and Lila recently had five more puppies.

In our family photo albums, there are now more people who aren't here than those who are. But I've also met new babies from new mothers, and my friends have children now who play with mine on shady afternoons in the summertime. My son calls me mamá now, and that strangeness I felt when I first got here has dissipated because there's something vital that transcends us and reaches them. The love of seeing the color of the sky in the place you were born, feeling the passing of the hours of the day as they are only felt here, the birds in the morning, the extended family and the inevitable closeness with those with whom we share a great part of life.

* * *

A cane you no longer use, a bar of soap, your spray deodorant, the adjustable orthopedic bed with the anti-decubitus mattress patched a thousand times, a pink quilt from the eighties and the red emergency bell hanging from a small cord next to you.

Your roommate's TV is so loud that it intrudes on my thoughts; you make it clear that it only bothers me, everyone else here is deaf. We laugh.

I brought you pastries, a few bars of dark chocolate, and raisins. And also a pad of unlined paper, and a box of colored pencils. I remembered when I was a kid you always brought me boxes of pencils and a box of alfajores when you were going away.

I sat next to you as you were drawing; you were having trouble curling your fingers around your pencil. You were gripping it too high up, and the tip of the pencil was barely grazing the sheet. I filmed you. I sat silently beside you watching how you went along with what seemed to be a landscape of a mountain town. We stayed like that for a while without making attempts to talk, without questions or exchange.

You were fine, at ease.

I cut your hair, your nails, I shaved you. We shared a cup of tea, I told you about my children; you couldn't hold them. You looked at them as if from far away and called the youngest by your brother's name. It seemed as though it brought something back to you because you told me about yourself, about your childhood, and about Rodolfo's insomnia, and you told me about the movie with the boy who had little jingle bells attached to his ankle so people could tell when he was running away. You also told me about your mother. You'd never really talked about her, and your eyes got bright when you said her name: Niní. You told me about the chocolate sponge cake she made and how she would embroider tablecloths by hand. Your fingers caressed the threads protruding from the fabric while I held your cup of tea.

You told me how she was a good woman and very sweet, how she lived for her children, but a bit more for her husband who'd found in her a familial love he'd never had before.

I saved a little black sweater knitted by my grandmother Niní that I take out every winter. When I do, I think of the things that are left behind, passed down between us from those who are no longer here.

* * *

When I went outside to leave, the icy cold made my ears throb. I felt it and breathed it in deep as if it would pass through my entire being and cleanse me of it all. I didn't put on my coat.

I waited for the bus under a plane tree with orange autumn leaves that's over two hundred years old. Water was flowing down the irrigation canal. I put on Neil Young. I waited for the No. 6 bus on the gravel on the other side of the curb from the street. I rode through the city on that bus, something I'd not done for so many years. I considered my age; I was in my twenties. I felt young.

It was my birthday, and everyone told me I looked young.

In that place where you are, the heat was turned all the way up. The smell of the unventilated space and disinfectant and all that sorrow stuck to the tip of my nostrils. As I ride this bus, I let my head loosely move from side to side against the seat. I look out the window at the streets I knew, and I think how time has passed. I remember you sitting there like in a photo: still, stiffly seated upright at the long table waiting for lunch at eleven o'clock in the morning with other people just as mute as you in that endless continuum of waiting for the next meal, a nap, tea, dinner, and to sleep and nothing else.

I come back here.

I think of how nice it is to live in such a quiet place; people are friendly and never in a hurry. That's what my little boy said, he notices everything, the little booger.

And there, in my face reflected back at me in that city bus window, I see you. We look alike: the skinny face, the high cheekbones, the shape of the nose. Also a little in the shape and color of our eyes. I stayed with you there, sitting in that dining room, your shoes untied because why not, your hand slumped on the arm of your wheelchair. You are only recognizable by the way your glasses sit on the tip of your nose and the look of effort you make to peer over them.

This time you were calmer and more settled, and that made you even more sad.

Ghosts come and go, same as always. You told me you were mad because this man called Washington was now your roommate and he's a fascist: "He used to work at ESMA," you said. The illegal detention center in Buenos Aires you were referring to closed in 1983. I told you it couldn't be since that old man's from Huaco, a town in the middle of the countryside of San Juan, but you said no, he's a torturer who goes around bragging about it, typical *milico*, and you should see how he treats the nurses, you said, then I'd understand.

Those ghosts of that horrible past kept on eating away at your mind.

Sometimes I would see you sitting there, in silence, staring into nothingness and I felt like rushing to save you from that dark place you'd gone. I thought of you, you in despair.

I sat on a concrete bench in the middle of a public plaza and looked at the sky, bluer than ever, and cried. I took a picture of you in the depth of that midday sky and thought about how the idea of coming back and you not being here no longer scares me.

* * *

We said goodbye. Sleet fell. I tucked you in with your down blanket and gave you a kiss.

I told you I would come back when it was warmer, I told you to look forward to it.

You said, like you always did, that when you were better, you were going to get on a plane and come see me. We laughed, without any sadness.

In the bathroom, my son looked at his black eye in the mirror, fresh from a schoolyard fight, and said he had no tears left.

It felt like an appropriate time to say that.

* * *

I dream a lot.

I dream that I'm walking through thick vegetation in a swamp filled with plants that aren't so tall, only a little taller than me, maybe. There is white pampas grass and mud all around and the grass scrapes against my leg, there, on my tibia. And it hurts, it burns, I bleed, and I grab my leg but I don't stop moving forward. I don't understand why I'm stuck there, lost, dying of heat, covered in mud and sweat, but as I advance there are voices in the distance that become more and more clear as I forge ahead. There's a group of people, maybe, at least I think there is, and I try to go to them, but I don't know where I'm going, because I'm just walking forward while brushing plants out of my face and pulling little things out of my hair and bugs off my clothes, and all of a sudden one leg sinks into the cold, sticky mud. A shiver runs down my spine and I take the next step. Now the other leg is sinking too, and I'm rooted up to my knees, sinking deeper, deeper.

I breathe and despair.

I lay back and start to move my legs as if I were a frog swimming. I try holding onto a rock for support, but it's no use. It's no use. I feel like some sort of clumsy scorpion, or worse, an insect on its back, useless. I think of the image of pilgrims approaching the reliquary, heaving themselves up the stairs. Why am I thinking about that now? I have to concentrate. I try to move my legs again now, but the clay is hardening around them like cement, and I scream so that those people I heard over there come to my rescue but my voice doesn't come out and again I despair. So, I take a breath, filling my lungs once more, and I scream again and there I wake up. I sit up in bed as if I were coming out of the swamp and my legs are asleep.

I change position.

I'm still in the swamp, but now I'm able to walk. It's a little muddy but I move gracefully, as if I know what I'm doing. At the high point I can see the mountains, with the sun setting they're half pink, half violet, and it must be spring because the temperature is still pleasant, and beyond I can see Alpha Canis Majoris, behind the Sierra Chica. I point out the Tres

Marías, laughing that the one in the middle is mine, but I'm not really sure who I'm talking to. The voices are nearer now but I keep passing through the plants, moving them aside with my hands, and the height of the plants shelters our movement in a kind of cool protective shade that feels very pleasant on my skin. We walk a bit more and now we hear something nice like jazz music, and something stings my left arm. I bring my right hand quickly to it. It hurts, it burns, I kill it, a horsefly, I shake it, I killed it and now the music's getting louder and there's screaming. A baby is crying. It looks so small and cries in distress and I try to move as fast as possible in some direction but even as I yank and I yank plants out of my way, the brush seems infinite and the baby's cries are becoming more and more intense and there's a woman who's also screaming and it's suffocating and I am desperate to get out of there and get to the other side, but now the mud is getting wetter and I begin to sink and it's colder, darker, and the plants block the view in front of me and I'm able to shake the mud off but I am still stuck, and now everything is silent.

Alpha Canis Majoris is above me, looking down at me, twinkling, glowing like it always does. I don't know why that brings me some peace, but I feel that I'm on the right planet. I don't get agitated anymore. I keep moving forward and when I run through the gnarled branches in front of me, the woman with the baby, who is no longer crying, looks at me with the biggest eyes I've ever seen, and I realize she is me.

I jolt awake. There is a halo of perspiration where I laid on my mattress, and my arms are itchy and swollen. The power is out, and the ceiling fan has stopped running.

I walk to the bathroom to get a glass of water. I pee half asleep and my phone buzzes. It's three in the morning. A message at three in the morning means something's wrong.

So many miles away and I'm covered in mud.

The days that follow are filled with anguish, uncertainty, paperwork, phone calls, family members you lost touch with in 1998, banks, bills to pay.

Your signature and thousands of pages of incomplete paperwork. Siblings and half-siblings scattered in different cities, some never having met one another, gather together.

Your last passport photo in my wallet and the wool poncho now splayed over my feet.

Dialogues

A SELECTION OF POEMS FROM *DIÁLOGOS*
(EXTRAMUROS, 2014) BY RAMÓN HONDAL

TRANSLATED BY ELENA LAHR-VIVAZ

ONE

It enters
Filters   buries the voice
Erases one signature with another.

What it buries
No body underground
Without voice
One signature atop another
The water filters the flesh
And what it was to the ground.

In the water
A drain beneath
Not the dirtiness
The gestures flow down

Through the water the skin
Drains down beneath the coolness.

The curtain pushed back   It emerges
Dries the skin
Halts that touch
Falls —Drips—
The grayness falls
Filtered

Look. They open their eyes. They awaken.

Begin to follow the gestures. Follow the first of the day.

Small tangling of words. The first of the day. Each gesture
    counts for later. Count them.

From the moment they open their eyes, count. Carefully.
    Always from afar.

You will hear the voice, the hushed voice, and never your
    own. Close yourself off and make room only for them.

Enter. Eyes open.

—To begin.

—What is this about?

—Would you want this?

—And the step.

—Tongueless? Voiceless? How?

—The light. The same gesture.

—Everything entangled. Never everything.

—A desire. Another.

—And the pressure of the body on the bed.

—About what?

The slow step. The quick one. Follow them. One by one,
    the steps.
Pay attention to the steps. The step resolves the voice.
    They go. And there is the unseen difference.
    The gesture.
The slow step, the quick. It corners.
The others pass. Ahead. Behind.
They go. Follow them. Follow just them.

—The other is slow.
—A hurry? A rush?
—The heat slows one down. . .
—A shadow.
—. . .and the heat is outside.
—A step isn't possible.
—The street is the same.
—Confined in the street.
—The leg in the tongue. Quiet.
—I step. I advance. I deny.

Hurry up. Slow down. Each at their own pace.

Each with their own map. Or a new one. For two. A
map that dies in the separation of four feet. At that
rhythm. At that other rhythm. Fast. Slow. A slip. A
fright. The street. Danger.

Enter by two. Enter with four feet. Forget your own map.
Your street.

Go to these two. You don't count.

Run. Hurry up. Slow down.

—One step is not possible.

—The heat.

—This street.

—To sit, where?

—The hole.

—The curb, and a slip.

—Because of the blind step, a fall.

—And the dust washed on the foot.

—The bench. The bed.

—Time to return.

Go out. Look.

There they are. In a wide-open space. The blended voice.
    Among everyone. The blended voice. Never everyone.
    They move, and the last step now is a park.

There they are. In an open space.

Look.

—It's nice without walls.

—A tree.

—It's a nice day.

—And the tongue, quiet on the foot.

—The gaze, and the voice inside.

—Entangled.

—This bench.

—So much heat. More than within the walls.

—The word on this bench.

—A slip of the tongue.

Look on that bench. In the park. There they are.

No one there, since there is no speech. Others pass by, and everyone. Never everyone. The bench outside, the wall inside.

Air. An open space. Closed up all the same. Before the room, now a park. The bed. The bench. A word. The same word. Two. Inside or out.

Look on the bench. Go out.

—How?

—I would want this . . .

—About what?

—There is a voice here.

—The tree trips over his foot.

—On this bench.

—Where it is clear.

—Above.

—And where language blends.

—About what?

They say goodbye. They continue. Toward a place. Let's
continue.

The step through the city. Encounters between walls.
The same place, inside or out. A space of voice and
entanglement. That which was said before was not
said.

But come on. Move. Let's continue.

—Language in emptiness.

—Hunger.

—A park with voices.

—A foot, entangled in the bench.

—And everything connected.

—It rubs against the skin.

—One progresses.

—Attack that step. Not yours.

—False. Everything. Never everything.

—There is doubt.

—The tongue. For what?

—The doubt, and the voice.

Enter into that which shatters. To one that sustains two.
Hard and split shaft. The support broken. The night and
    another language. Look. Occupy. You occupy. Broken.
Enter. Look. Touch.

—The night outside.
—A guitar. A trumpet.
—Connected.
—Voiceless.
—This foot, with tongue.
—Too much light. Not outside.
—The black resounds.
—The voice entangled, and the tone.
—To swallow each cord. To fail.
—The gaze that I do not have.
—The foot that was born below.
—The guitar. The trumpet. Accompanying voices.

They eat. They talk. They wait. Look.

Look, while they wait. Take a seat. Inhabit. Lift your leg
  onto the table. Walk on the table.

A gesture. They talk. Everything entangled on the table.
  Not everything. One knows. It repeats. They are.

There, two talk, one. There they are. Enter.

—There is a covered hole.

—Too cold.

—Relief from the emptiness and fatigue. Weariness.

—The cold inside. . .

—Some shelter.

—. . . and the heat outside.

—The room. Go to the room and stay.

—But to go out in the heat. . .

—Stay.

—. . . breaks the voice.

Look.

One wants to.

The other does not.

The difference is erased with the desire to repeat.

Look. It's over.

And one remains.

The weariness returns. From within. Keep walking.
  Watch.
The voice denies and erases the word. Enter this voice.
  Listen to it. Listen where the voice remains. Nothing
  and everything in it. And thus, the doubt. Possible to
  be outside, from within. Enter and look.
When the two see each other, deny them. Deny them
  there. And look.

—This voice tires.
—But the step is usually there. Firm.
—Well, the voice itself.
—Everything not so clear. No.
—Between which things the weariness?
—Never clarity between two.
—In silence. The voice within.
—And the tongue becomes twisted.
—Or afterwards. . .

Look. That's how words become voice.

Enter. Enter into the weariness. The rhetoric of sentences, their stubbornness. And it becomes confused. Look again. Look carefully.

—Where is it?
—Or after.
—I would like this but. . .
—Yes, something but not everything.
—Never everything.
—Things go wrong.
—About what? Not first.
—That they don't know. . .

One has to enter, follow, and choose. Don't be still. Look
   at them.

There are various rooms. Through this one, yes. This one,
   no. Follow the voice. That which can be heard. One.
   Two. Three voices. From one place. From one throat.
   There. You must continue.

Enter. Look.

—Something but not everything.

—The tongue. The tongue.

—Never everything.

—The foot. The foot.

—And to take the first step.

—Things go wrong.

—Yes, with the other.

—The silence within. And this body.

—Erase the other. Erase his voice.

—I see.

—And yours.

—This body.

TO SAY. . .

To lose words
To not write
To be left split in half
To speak
Fever
To speak
Says the half.

The density of half
The communication
The scarcity of letters
The excess
A time to organize
Not to do it.

To say. . .

Mere Diary

A BILINGUAL SELECTION FROM *DIARIO ÍNFIMO*
(EDICIONES DE LA ISLA DE SILTOLÁ, 2016)
BY MERCEDES ROFFÉ

TRANSLATED BY LUCINA SCHELL

19 de mayo
REMINISCENCIAS

hoy en el cielo hubo fuegos
y grises
y algún jirón rosado
desplegándose
sobre el río brumoso
—su horizonte

hoy fue un día de luces
y sorna y farsa
y algún mirar fastidiado

un desencuentro

un libro que alguien dejó   caer en tus manos
una pregunta
una espera

hoy   quienquiera que fuese
leyó como si amara
en la palabra el alma que la intuye
o labra
o borronea

hoy alguien susurró
al oído de alguien
un poema improbable
incierto

receloso

como una garúa

May 19
REMINISCENCES

today in the sky there were fires
and grays
and some pink rag
unfurling
over the murky river
—its horizon

today was a day of lights
and sarcasm and farse
and an annoyed look

a disagreement

a book that someone let   fall into your hands
a question
a waiting

today   whoever it was
read as if she loved
the soul in the word that senses
or works
or scrawls it

today someone whispered
into someone's ear
an improbable
uncertain poem

distrustful

like a drizzle of rain

22 de mayo
PASOS

entonces la manera de empezar
es remontarse

desandar cada senda
cada atajo
la hierba herida donde el pie ha pisado
el surco que la aparta y enajena
de la mitad de sí

pero esta vez no fallar
no distraerse
no perdonarse ni el error ni el olvido

otros serán error y olvido
que los habrá

error y olvido

el hueco
donde todo lo demás respira y mama
el desvío
donde todo lo demás

llega a ser lo que es

como volver a las cosas que
alguna vez
alguien nos dijo en un sueño
—ese retrato rotundo
la voz del sueño
encarnada en quien no es sino
símbolo
de sí mismo
su propia cifra
mascullando siempre una verdad
destinada a extraviarse

esa traducción
siempre perfecta
fallida siempre
profética de lo que jamás
entenderemos
de lo que nunca entendimos

May 22
STEPS

then the way to begin
is to look back

unwalk each path
each shortcut
the injured grass where the foot has stepped
the track that divides and alienates it
from its other half

but this time not to fail
or get distracted
or forgive oneself errors or erasures

different errors and erasures
will be made

errors and erasures

the hole
where everything else breathes and suckles
the detour

where everything else
becomes what it is

like returning to the things that
at one time
someone told us in a dream
—that plump portrait

the voice from the dream
embodied in those who are but
symbols
of themselves
their own cipher
always muttering a truth
destined to go astray

that translation
always perfect
failed always
a prophecy of what we'll never
understand
of what we never understood

7 de julio
LULLABY

Oh hermosa luna de papel
baja a jugar con nosotros

somos
dos árboles solitarios
anclados
en un paisaje
de hierro y lodo

(SILENCIO)

*

Oh luna de papel de arroz
¿por qué nos miras
severa
desde lo alto?

¿qué nos reclamas?

¿es nuestra culpa si
en este paraje
hostil

hirsuto
fuimos abandonados?

(SILENCIO)

*

Mala luna de cobre
sanguinolenta luna

vete

nos vence el miedo
y ni siquiera huir
podemos
varados como estamos
en este yermo
valle   oscuro
desolado

(SILENCIO)

July 7
LULLABY

Oh beautiful paper moon
come down and play with us

we are
two solitary trees
anchored
in a landscape
of iron and mud

(SILENCE)

*

Oh rice paper moon
why do you look on us
sternly
from up high?

what do you ask of us?

is it our fault if
in this hostile
thorny

spot
we were abandoned?

(SILENCE)

*

Evil copper moon
bloodshot moon

be gone

fear overcomes us
and we can't even
flee
stranded as we are
in this barren
dark   desolate
valley

(SILENCE)

27 de julio
MUJERES DE NEGRO

bolsa al hombro
—cuando no nosotras
dentro

y la soledad cada cual
como puede
—algunas, bajo el brazo
otras
quebrándole la cadera
otra, hundiéndose
a lo lejos

¿es un río?
mujeres son
—dicen

¿un río somos?
a lo más un arroyo

y las casitas allá
alineadas

tan prolijitas
y ese mundo
aun más atrás
tan alto
y fuego
y noche

Pero ellas van mirándose
la punta de los zapatos

no alzar la vista
ni la voz
podría decirse
su esencia

bajo la luz de una lámpara color miel
lee
fuma
bebe
un señor en su bata
de seda azul

de las anchas solapas
sacude
—soplando apenas—
una brizna dorada

July 27
WOMEN IN BLACK

Bags shouldered
—when it's not us
inside them

and the loneliness each
as best she can
—one, under her arm
another
thrusting her hip
another, sinking
in the distance

is it a river?
it's women
—they say

are we a river?
a stream at most

and the little houses there
all lined up
meticulously

and that world
even further beyond
so tall
and fire
and night

But they go on looking
down at their toes

not raising their gaze
nor voice
it could be said
their essence

under the honey-colored lamplight
reads
smokes
drinks
a fine sir in his robe
of blue silk

from the wide lapels
he brushes off
—barely blown—
a golden thread

20 de agosto
CAMINO RURAL

en ellas
el grito
es aún más silencio

August 20
RURAL JOURNEY

the cry
in those women
is even more silence

3 de septiembre
DECISIONES

digamos
que no quieres
pero
que te encuentras
en una situación en que
pero
no quieres

más aun:
digamos que
ni siquiera
      te parecería aceptable

que aceptar
algo así
sería

pero digamos que
sientes
  (oh sí
      cuánto cuánto
  lo sientes)

pero   digamos que
acabas de aceptarlo
en-nombre-de

September 3
DECISIONS

let's say
you don't want to
but
you find yourself
in a situation in which
but
don't want to

what's more:
let's say
it wouldn't even
         seem acceptable to you

that to accept
something like that
would be

but let's say
you feel
   (oh yes
         how very
   badly you feel)

but   let's say
you just accepted it
in-name-of

16 de septiembre
PATIO INTERIOR

eso no era una fiesta
ni una reunión de amigos

bajo un sol tan extremo
se adivinaba algo turbio

las aves picaban migajas
que les habían echado
lejos
como por distraerlas

Y en eso fue que llegaron ellas
severas
firmes
implacables

tal vez sombrías

Pero definitivamente esos niños
no debían
estar allí

September 16
INNER COURTYARD

that was not a party
nor a gathering of friends

under a blazing sun
something shady was at work

the birds pecked crumbs
that had been scattered
far away
as if to distract them

And suddenly those women arrived
stern
determined
ruthless

perhaps somber

But certainly those children
weren't supposed
to be there

22 de octubre
PRIMAVERA GRIS

Confiesa que lo has bordado
muy de prisa
a gigantescas puntadas
como si te corrieran
como las Brontë

¿por eso
la casa atrás?
    ¿siempre irrumpiendo
    la casa
    —urgiéndote,
    asediando?

tan frágiles los árboles
que un viento leve los vence

tan ominoso y certero
el vuelo de las aves

October 22
GRAY SPRING

Admit that you've embroidered it
hurriedly
with gigantic stitches
like you were being chased
like the Brontë sisters

is that why
the house behind?
       always the house
       bursting in
       —urging,
       pestering you?

so delicate the trees
a light wind bends them

so ominous and unerring
the birds' flight

15 de noviembre
LA AVENIDA

si hay árboles como hojas

si hay gente
como signos de admiración

también ha de haber, seguramente

mundos
como avenidas radiantes
ocres
niñas

cielos
como dorados cúmulos preñados
transparentes

galaxias, cosmos, éteres
como negros carruajes

November 15
THE AVENUE

if there are trees like leaves

if there are people
like exclamation points

there must also be, surely

worlds
like radiant ochre
girly
avenues

skies
like golden bulging
transparent cumuli

galaxies, cosmos, ethers
like black carriages

27 de noviembre
COLOR-WRITING, 1

ZA ZA ZA ZA ZA UMMMM
za za za za za ummmm

grita
balbucea
la mistérica
glándula
pineal

inserta como un blanco la palabra
justo
en el descentro
de ese trono del alma
o Ajna
o punto
ciego
órgano
del temblor

sanguinolento avatar
iluminado y necio
el ojo

celestial
un poco estrábico un poco
hermano
de aquel sonriente pólipo
de Redon
que mira absorto
siempre
al infinito
y aun sonriendo un poco
siempre
un poco
como la muerte

November 27
COLOR-WRITING, 1

ZA ZA ZA ZA ZA UMMMM
za za za za za ummmm

it cries
it babbles
the mysterical
pineal
gland

embedded like a target the word
right
in the off-center
of that throne of the soul
or Ajna
or blind
spot
organ
of tremor

bloodshot avatar
enlightened and dimwitted
the celestial

eye
a bit squinty a bit
kindred
to that smiling polyp
of Redon
that stares engrossed
always
toward the infinite
and smiling a bit
always
a bit
like death

2 de diciembre
FÁRRAGOS

a veces
¿no es también el silencio
discursivo en exceso?

December 2
JUMBLES

sometimes
isn't silence also
excessively verbose?

3 de diciembre
COLOR-WRITING, 2

anotar en la tela

luego

un azul clásico noche
—cielo de luna llena—
un naranja de cadmio claro,
intenso

irregularidades

palabras gris-grafito
deslizándose

círculo
contenedor y dudosa
flecha
adoctrinando

—He de morir de estas cosas —dijo,
pensando
en la antigua sombra
de una flor que declina

December 3
COLOR-WRITING, 2

to take notes on the canvas

later

a classic night blue
—full moon sky—
an orange of pale,
intense cadmium

irregularities

gray-graphite words
slipping

containing
circle and doubtful
arrow
indoctrinating

"I should die of these things,"
she said, thinking
of the ancient shadow
of a drooping flower

13 de diciembre
REGRESOS

incuba el viaje

duerme

honra

lo que te ha sido dado vislumbrar

vuelve

pregúntales por qué

para qué

acepta

la antigua

la nueva travesía

December 13
RETURNS

incubate the journey

sleep

honor

what has been given to you to discern

return

ask them why

for what

accept

the old

the new voyage

17 de diciembre
COLOR-WRITING, 3

en cambio aquí hay estudio

un tiempo
de meditar y medir
las consecuencias

un círculo arrebolado o
casi
y otro círculo dentro
y otro adentro
y otro

solo esa aguja fija, excéntrica
nos alerta
como queriendo
dar la ilusión
de un nuevo orden
más lábil
más perfecto

December 17
COLOR-WRITING, 3

by contrast here there is study

a time
to meditate and measure
the consequences

a reddened circle or
sort of
and another circle inside
and inside it another one
and another

only that static, eccentric needle
alerts us
as if wanting
to give the illusion
of a new order
more labile
more perfect

25 de diciembre
SANGRE

extraño
¿no?
que un engaño
confirme
una verdad

December 25
BLOOD

odd
isn't it?
that a fraud
would verify
a truth

NOTE

The poems entitled "Color-Writing, 1, 2, and 3" are based on three works by the Russian painter Olga Rozanova; "Women in Black" and "Rural Journey" are based on homonymous works by Marianne von Werefkin; "Inner Courtyard," "Gray Spring," and "The Avenue" were inspired by works of the same title by Alice Bailly. Different versions of these poems were published alongside the artworks that inspired them in an anthology of Roffé's ekphrastic poetry titled *The Radiance of Things* (Shearsman Books, 2022), as a free e-book only: https://www.shearsman.com/poetry-books-e-books. The poem "Lullaby" arose from a visual artwork that the poet hasn't managed to locate again.

Smoke Shrouds the Earth

AN EXCERPT OF *EL HUMO SOBRE LA TIERRA* (ERDOSAIN EDICIONES, 2016) BY MANUEL ARDUINO PAVÓN

ILLUSTRATED BY BLANCO PANTOJA AND TRANSLATED BY SARA LISSA PAULSON

I. IN THE BEGINNING

I am a simple man. As simple as a wicker basket.

Due to some unknown cause, my wicker basket caught fire.

I was at home in the garden, next to the golden pool.[1]

I didn't have any source of fire in my hands, nor was the sun shining down rampantly. Nothing could justify the fact that my wicker basket was burning.

I went inside to get a blanket to smother the fire. I have always been afraid of the unleashed fury of fire.

---

1. Translator's note: The Spanish word *pileta* can also signify font, pit, pond, basin, washbasin, or the puddling of water in a mine.

When I returned to the garden, the wicker basket had been reduced to a pile of solid, charred remains and a little smoke—an insignificant ring of pitch-black smoke.

The smoke reached my body, the only place on earth it shouldn't have. Transfixed, I watched how the smoke curled over my right hand and right there I witnessed a prodigy of nature: on my right hand a giant mosquito arose out of nowhere, a giant mosquito over two inches long.

I was terrified.

The mosquito swiftly threatened to sting the back of my hand. Violently, I flicked it off.

Then it buzzed around and flew away.

I looked at the basket, or what was left of it. There was no more smoke.

Such a paucity of smoke after this inexplicable fire?

An inexplicable mosquito of such sinister dimensions rising out of an inconceivable swirl of smoke?

I wanted to forget it all: I would buy another wicker basket.

But this basket had been a gift from the chief of the Laguna Verde people.

I would never find another one like it.

For a split second, I wondered if the chief had woven a spell into it.

*   *   *

At nightfall, I thought I heard my neighbor calling me.

I waved at him through the window.

"I just killed an enormously massive mosquito!"

"About two inches long, right?"

"Two inches? More like six!"

That frightened me.

"They say there are others on the block," my neighbor informed me.

I thought about the remains of the smoke, the remains of the smoke traveling through the air.

"How many?"

"Only one more. For now, only one."

"Alive or dead?"

"The native didn't kill it. But he saw one fly by. I think that's what happened."

"That's odd."

"It's awful. Humanity is to blame. It's because of all those crazy experiments."

I didn't breathe a word about the smoke. I thought about the ancient peoples of Laguna Verde, about our human ancestry.

I didn't mention the basket that had spontaneously combusted. I didn't breathe a word about that.

It was too much for one single night.

We parted ways.

*   *   *

My bedroom window was illuminated by the white glow of the moon. An intense opalescent radiation penetrated the crystals of the window, lending a magic aura to the room.

Lying in bed, I beheld a disconcerting and outrageous spectacle.

Just as I was closing my eyes, I heard a violent flapping of wings hitting the windowpane.

An enormous mosquito, the size of a cat, hovered outside.

I jumped up.

I got my rifle, always at my bedside.

I slid open the window and aimed. The moonlight allowed me to easily pinpoint my target.

I fired.

The colossal mosquito fell to the ground, right next to my neighbor's fence.

I put my robe on and went out to the garden, rifle in hand.

I walked over to the fence.
Repulsed, I watched as two other giant mosquitos circled around the ones lying dead.

I finished them off with two more sure shots.

The noise woke up my neighbor.

"They are bigger now!" he said, terrified.

"Yes, it seems like they are growing bigger and bigger. We must find a way to trap them before they transform into something even more horrifying."

"Watch out!" he yelled, pushing me to the ground.

I looked up. Two more mosquitos were coming right at us.

I took the rifle and shot.

I was a good hunter: they fell like heavy sacks of coal.

It looked like the worst had happened: the pitch-black smoke, though small in quantity, had given life to creatures that kept growing and sowing panic.

I wondered if the mosquitos might be hovering around their birthplace, the original wisp of smoke.

*   *   *

I thought to myself that there must be some substance in the withies of the charred basket.

I resolved not to say a word about the incident, about the burning basket. I was afraid that all the accusations would fall on me. I knew what men were like. As much as or more than I knew what giant mosquitos were like. There was very little difference.

The moonlight high above still held sway.

I had an idea.

I went to get the carbonized remains of the basket. Maybe there resided a power in the remains—in this case the power to lure the horrific mosquitos.

In secret, after loading my rifle, I slipped into the shadowy garden with the charred basket.

Naturally, I placed the remains next to the giant mosquito corpses.

I noticed that the basket didn't have any smell of being burnt.

It surprised me that I hadn't noticed it before.

It was truly bizarre: in a handful of hours, the basket smelled of nothing at all.

* * *

I did not allow my imagination to fly into some inscrutable zone or allow suspicion and delirium to torture me more than reality.

And I decided to lay aside for another time the problem of the chief, the shaman, and the Laguna Verde.

The moment I stopped fixating on myself and my next steps, I heard the atrocious buzzing of mosquitos resume.

I ran to tell my neighbor, who was gazing at the sky from a distant window.

I screamed that the mosquitos were coming closer.

This time there were about eight or nine of them.

We shot them directly above the charred basket.

I could no longer hide the obvious.

My neighbor seemed curious about the burnt remains and their magnetic power.

I told him everything that had to do with the spontaneous combustion and the spontaneous smoke.

*   *   *

From my perspective, I reasoned that since the first giant mosquito had emerged from the smoke, the others must have come out of the remaining smoke.

My neighbor reassured me that, except for the mosquito his neighbor had seen a few blocks away, there had been no other signs of anything out of the ordinary in the entire village.

I wanted to know more about that neighbor so I initiated a brief investigation.

"He is indigenous, you know, mestizo. He is from Laguna Verde."

Those words caught my attention.

My neighbor didn't know as many details about this indigenous man as I would have liked.

But he shared other thoughts about the charred basket and the smoke that had emanated from it.

*   *   *

He said quite reasonably that, except for some kind of spell or magic ritual, there was no way on earth that the charred basket and its smoke could have given birth to such creatures.

I had no choice but to open the doors of my mind to him.

I told him about the chief shaman of Laguna Verde, and how he had given me that basket as a present.

My neighbor wanted to know under what circumstances he had presented me with the gift.

My memory was foggy, but I thought it was the result of a conflict having been resolved between the lumber company where I worked some years ago and the people of Laguna Verde.

I had worked as a liaison between the company and the people of Laguna Verde due to my knowledge of their language. No one else had come with me to that meeting; I was the only one who had left the rainforest with a wicker basket, woven by the chief.

"Evidently that chief shaman has supernatural powers of alarming magnitude."

*   *   *

We carried the new corpses of the horrific creatures over to the remains of the charred basket in between the two houses. We placed everything in range of our respective guns.

"We should take turns keeping watch. Go lie down. I will phone you at five o'clock and you can take my place."

I was very tired and I needed to sleep. I accepted his proposition.

*   *   *

There are opportunities in life to abandon what is at hand and surrender oneself to the free-flowing night. Moments when we should trust in nothing more than the healing power of nighttime.

II. IN THE BEGINNING

I could barely close my eyes. The sounds of unrestrained chanting rose up from the garden and filled my bedroom, under the full moon's dutiful blanket of light.

I leaned out the window.

There was my neighbor, rifle in hand, and a shirtless man dancing around the giant mosquito corpses and my charred wicker basket.

I put on my bathrobe and ran downstairs, not forgetting my rifle.

When I was about to approach the stranger, my neighbor explained:

"He is the one from Laguna Verde, the one who found the giant mosquito three blocks from here."

"But what is he doing?"

"He believes these mosquitos are gods of the Laguna Verde people."

I remembered those creatures bursting out of the smoke from the handwoven basket, spontaneously and magically, as if they were gods. The native's apparent frenzy made some kind of sense.

I attempted to talk to him in a language closely related to his own.

I asked him to explain what the dance meant.

Slowly I began to understand that it was a ritual dance, a sort of propitiatory dance.

I mentioned that to my neighbor.

"To propitiate for what?" he asked, somewhat perplexed.

"He didn't elaborate. It's odd."

I asked him if he knew how many gods of Laguna Verde, in the form of giant mosquitos, were among us now.

His answer surprised me.

While he danced without ceasing, he said though many mosquitos were dead, it was certain that not many were gods.

I didn't understand this paradox.

I persisted with my question.

From his perspective, and in accordance with his lateral thinking, he explained that sometimes gods make other beings appear as gods even though they are not, that sacred mosquitos usually number seven, and only seven, and that gods assume apparently illusory shapes to disorient the world's inhabitants.

This account calmed my nerves: a mere seven mosquitos with power.

I shared the native man's exact words with my neighbor.

The Coming Desert

A SELECTION OF POEMS FROM *EL PRÓXIMO DESIERTO*
(EDITORIAL UNIVERSIDAD DE GUADALAJARA, 2019)
BY SANTIAGO ACOSTA

TRANSLATED BY TIFFANY TROY AND THE WOMEN IN TRANSLATION
PROJECT AT THE UNIVERSITY OF WISCONSIN-MADISON

DEAD HORSE BAY

1.

One morning I left home and took the Q35 down to
    Brooklyn.

On the phone, the blue path showed me the way to
    Barren Island, a man-made peninsula that sits on an
    old landfill.

I got off just before the bridge that leads to the less
    popular shores of Queens.

The path to the bay was narrow and overgrown.

I was cold, but filled with desire.

A rounded stone stood out among the bushes as the only
vestige of a wheat mill built by Dutch settlers in the
seventeenth century.

The beach was a trove of objects sprouting out of the
ground.

Countless bottles, frayed rags, shoe soles, toy parts,
rusted frames covered in sargasso.

What had I come to look for within this garbage heap?

What was I doing in this place, cutting my fingers with
the debris of another time?

2.

*Green bottles. Amber bottles. Crystalline bottles. Broken
bottles.*

*Bleach bottles. Bottles from the nineteenth century. Bottles
from the twentieth century.*

Perfume bottles and bottles of nail polish. Medicine bottles.
Bourbon bottles.

Bottles that belonged to artists and bottles that belonged to
high school teachers.

Bottles of the Federal government. Bottles of displaced
immigrants. Bottles of arsenic.

3.

The entire afternoon I wandered the beach with
collectors, photographers, and treasure hunters.

Shivering, I dug out from the rocks the miniature
porcelain head of a woman and some marbles, worn
down by the waves.

For a moment I was in a movie, the sole survivor of a
mass extinction.

To my left, the sea. To my right, the highway. At my feet,
the scene of an undeniable future.

With every storm, the sand spits out another layer of
refuse.

The following days bring new waves of visitors who
    believe beach cleanup is honorable labor.

(Someone must always keep in motion the cycle of
    objects.)

4.

*In the free circulation of commodities, there is no center or edge.
We are all part of the same untraceable sludge.*

*Lead from discarded batteries seeps into the water in the same
way that capital floods the landscapes of our childhood.*

*I want to be the first to digest this gigantic iceberg of nylon,
glass, and metal.*

This world modifies us, we are just one of its painful mutations.

5.

Before it turned into a landfill, there was a glue factory
    here.

Bodies of horses arrived from all parts of the city, having
    collapsed in the street after years of slavery and
    exhaustion.

To extract collagen, they boiled bones, hooves, skin, tendons, and cartilage. After repeating the procedure several times, a yellow paste was bottled and put on sale.

The rancid odor of the resulting fumes caused illness in the nearby working-class neighborhoods and could be felt even in the eastern reaches of the city.

It was in those years that the area gained the name of Dead Horse Bay.

Even today you can find cut femurs, broken jaws, or hip bones bleached by the sun.

6.

Bottles still intact under the sand and mud. Bottles covered in algae.

Bottles among the propellers of abandoned boats.

Bottles among the carcasses of manta rays. Bottles under the claws of horseshoe crabs.

The clink of bottles swaying in the tide.

This is the result of what we are, a land of glass
shattering with each downpour.

BONE BROTH

1.

The university had turned into a battlefield.

Police lights flickered patterns in the air thick with gas.

I took the last exit before the tunnel, and we descended
a zigzagging path.

On the roadside, concrete pillars precariously
supported houses above the ravine.

Makeshift drains, black cables, and remnants of posters
from the last election hung from balconies.

Out the car windows we could see lines of bulldozers
parked at the bottom of the valley, awaiting the final
order.

2.

We crossed mud and zinc in silence, searching the radio
for a station still airing.

These last days tasted like the toxic residue of a
controlled combustion.

Crowds of protesters tried to shut down the highway,
overturning a truck of cattle bones from the
slaughterhouse.

As food was scarce, nearby residents dismantled the
barricades and cooked them down into a broth.

I thought of the hallways of my school, vandalized and
engulfed in flames.

Someone said we no longer had any reason to go back.

We left the car behind a dumpster painted with the
Party's flag and the slogan: "I am the Ark of Life."

We felt our intestines burn from years of abusing alcohol
and sedatives.

We crossed sandy terraces on foot, away from the glow of
a city that finally turned its back on us.

3.

*So many years flying over cities in flames, without being
touched by the diamonds outside.*

*What did it mean to recognize, at this very moment, that
forgotten space?*

This is the border where hope and death reconcile.

4.

Those who welcomed us at their table did not realize they
were saving us from imminent death.

Bone broth—we later learned—has a long history of
therapeutic use.

Collagen extracted through boiling restores the intestinal
lining, so bone broth is the chosen elixir of digestive
ailments.

My head was spinning.

I remembered my father and my mother. And my brother.

Thirty million people in this city and we still can't trust anyone.

Bile rose up my throat like a geyser in the desert night.

5.

I woke up to another blackout.

The bang and rattle of the transformers announced an imminent ambush.

It was the latest tactic of law enforcement.

We quickly gathered our belongings, said goodbye, and headed into the deep valley.

No one said that every journey had to reach its end.

What we were planning was foolish, but to our ears the truth sounded like a cheap fabrication.

The Girl from Mexico

FROM *LA CASA CHICA* (PLANETA 2012) BY MÓNICA LAVÍN

TRANSLATED BY D. P. SNYDER

732 Rodeo Drive
Beverly Hills
Los Angeles

Lupe Vélez adored parties.

Maybe it was her way of feeling loved, of making the
good times so loud that she didn't have to think about all
the heartaches and hard work that had brought her to live
in that California-style mansion on Rodeo Drive. She drew
back the bedroom curtains and looked out at her garden.
How she loved the royal palm that towered majestically
in the middle of the big lawn! Her gaze traveled across
the rose bushes, the masses of azalea in one corner, the
vine climbing up the tree, the garage roof. And all of it was
hers, a half-acre garden that her mother could never have
dreamed of owning when her four daughters were small

and they all had to leave Mexico City. She had only seen
its equal at the San Antonio School. She used to think it
was so comical to see the nuns crossing the garden at Our
Lady of the Lake, looking like little white and gray dots, like
the wild rabbits don Braulio shot and brought home to be
stewed in colorín and chiles at General Jacobo Villalobos's
house, the old homestead in San Luis Potosí. Childhood felt
like a million years ago.

Lupe ran her hand across her flat belly. It wouldn't be
like that for long, she thought, and she didn't much like
the idea. She had not been happy to find out about the
pregnancy, and Harald was even less pleased when she told
him about it over dinner at the Brown Derby. All he said
was: Well, now you'll have to stop smoking, honey. And she
snapped back, and you'll have to get divorced. Because it's
yours. Whatever way you looked at it, thirty-four, or thirty-
six with the two years she'd been forced to add when she
came to work in the United States, was a little old to start
making babies. She lingered there at the windowsill: it was
December 13th and even though it was a day late, she was
throwing a party for her saint's day.

We'll celebrate La Virgen de Guadalupe, she told
Edelmira a month ago when she started planning it.

That sounds great, especially since you're not working
right now.

It was true: after the shoot in Mexico, no other projects

had come her way. War had darkened the horizon. Then, when she missed her period, she wanted to cancel the stupid party, even more so when Harald got so dodgy after hearing the news.

A piece of you. Your blood and my blood. Austrian and Mexican. A real doll.

You'd better stop drinking, was all he said.

Lupe would not stop drinking. She'd throw a real blowout so she could drink all day and night. Who wanted to be a single mother, an unmarried woman? To have a kid with the last name Vélez and thus to follow in the footsteps of her mother, who had kept using her maiden name even after she was married.

Book Jeff's band, she told Edelmira two months ago when they were having breakfast together on the terrace at the house.

Edelmira was her friend and her agent, and for some reason or another, she was also the person in charge of cheering Lupe up when she was down, which wasn't often. After the breakup with Arturo de Córdova, however, Lupe hadn't bounced back. That's why Edelmira went along with the idea of the party, took on the task of booking the musicians, and went on and on about the pozole that Rosita was going to make.

I don't want it to be a Mexican party. I want all my guests to have something they feel like eating.

But the truth was that the people who came to Lupe's place were the ones in the know: the food there was not garden variety. There, they went out of their way, seasoning a tender young goat with guacamole, green enchiladas, or an authentic mole.

Okay, so we'll serve other dishes, said Edelmira, giving in. Anyway, she knew that Lupe would forget all about the menu, anyway, as she always did, and focus on her part: writing the invitations, calling her friends, making decisions about the decorations and her outfit, and transforming her motley crowd into a swarm of revelers all enthralled by her energy, her wit, her unpredictable ripostes, and the songs that she'd wind up singing solo—or with whomever she chose.

Lupe dropped the curtain. Max had driven her car up to the house and she had to get ready to go out to buy the fresh flowers. They were never in short supply at her house, and she didn't leave that task to either Edelmira or Max, who was as clumsy at choosing flowers as he was good-looking. She wouldn't leave the task to Rosita's daughter either, because when she saw Max and his impressive, towering figure, the girl became completely flustered. She was so besotted by the chauffeur that she would wind up choosing the least interesting flowers. Yes, Max was handsome and why not? Lupe liked tall, strong men.

And if she was paying the salary, she'd give it to someone who was easy on the eyes. And if they happened to make her lovers jealous? All the better. After Johnny, none of them had moved in with her, anyway. She glanced at her watch. She'd have a quick coffee and then go upstairs and take a bath. She felt a little woozy. She was two-months pregnant and, even though her waistline was still slim, the lightheadedness she felt when she'd had nothing to eat was a reminder of her condition. Party, party, party, she thought to distract herself while she slipped on her robe and went down to the kitchen.

The Guest List

It wasn't going to be just any shindig. Champagne would be awaiting the guests the second they stepped in the door where there would be waiters to hand them a sparkling glass. Lupe told Edelmira how she wanted it all to go.

Are there enough champagne flutes? she asked.

There were enough for thirty-six guests. Lupe wanted to invite the same number of people as the age she claimed she was.

Afterward, you can have them, she said to Edelmira, who looked at her sternly. I don't think I'll be having any more parties. . . Or if I do, they'll be kiddie parties.

Edelmira, who knew her well, took note of the ironic tone of her comment. She tried to say something but Lupe changed the topic.

Today's a celebration, and we're not going to talk about anything else. Order my lunch, I'm going to leave soon, You take care of arranging the tables and organizing the waiters. This is where I want the musicians to be, she said, gesturing to the back of the living room. And tell Max to check all the lights in the garden. Also, I want to make a path with votive candles. I'll buy them when we go out.

A little fruit to start and a coffee rescued Lupe from her sensation of emptiness and lightheadedness. She devoured the banana pancake Rosita made for her.

Gary hasn't confirmed, said Edelmira. Do you want me to call him again, or do you want to do it?

I don't want him to show up with his wife, that bore. . . And he won't come alone. We know that, Edel.

It was you who insisted on inviting him. He's always watching out for you.

Well, it's not everybody who's named after the Virgin of Guadalupe.

She wanted Gary to come, to be there on her special day. She was gathering all the people she cared most about in that house that he had helped her buy. Mr. Sweet-Eyes, the most handsome man she'd ever laid eyes on. She should've been happy with the good fortune of being held in his arms during the filming of *The Wolf Song*, but then he got turned on, too. It wasn't hard to make that happen, as she later proved. But petite as she was, a chaparrita, all big-eyed and sassy, Mr. Cooper was bowled over by her. Those legs, that voice, that red mouth, that audacious personality, that love of life, her work ethic, those slender hips, and the way she purred when he caressed her. Gary Cooper had taken Lupe to the heights of love. How could she descend again to the land of mere mortals? Gary Cooper and Lupe Vélez. People talked, the sex and whiskey flowed, the movies were going from silent to talkies, and there was Lupe, who acted with her eyes, and sang, or danced with equal ease.

What good English, Gary said to her.

We Mexican girls learn from a young age.

I can see you do, he said, taking hold of her waist. I can see how very well you learn.

He was roguish and flirty, a sweet animal, a man who made women swoon. And he had been hers the minute she stepped foot in Hollywood. When mamá Josefina and her sister Mercedes visited Lupe, they couldn't believe the mansion she owned.

Mister Cooper helped me.

But *Mister* Cooper is married, warned doña Josefina, who was clever and knew her daughter was, too. Could he take it away from you? she ventured.

The house? Lupe laughed. No way! He's gonna come and live here.

That's what she thought back then. Gary would devote his life to her. He'd already shown his dedication with the magnificent gesture of helping her buy the house. But three years later, he gave her the cold shoulder. They didn't get married and stopped seeing each other. It had become too noisy for his wife and Cooper's mother. The chaparrita made too many demands on the actor, who could have any model or actress he wanted anyway.

You're never going to leave your wife. You don't have the guts, a resentful Lupe said.

And with that, she sealed her fate. Gary stayed married and went on to have many more affairs. The Hollywood gossip machine never stopped.

By the time she went upstairs to take her bath, she was sure of it. Gary wouldn't be coming to her party.

Bubble Bath

The bath was drawn. While she had breakfast, Rosita's daughter brought the water to the temperature she liked and added the jasmine-scented bath salts she preferred. She lived like a spoiled child, Lupe told herself, but her work had cost her dearly. What's more, the weariness that flooded her that day made her feel as if she'd grown

old before her time. Weariness in the skin, Lupe wanted
to say to the girl, but she kept quiet. In the skin, she said,
sliding her hand along her body surrounded by bubbles that
floated silently away. Sun poured through the bathroom
window and filled the tub with light, a private pleasure.
That day, though, she didn't feel like spending time on her
body, because it had stopped being just hers alone the day
another being became part of her flesh, there inside her
belly. It was overwhelming to think about: her bath had
stopped being her own habitual, intimate ritual and she
now bore the responsibility for a small being whose heart
was already beating and circulating blood around its little
body. She closed her eyes against the brightness of the day
as if it annoyed her. Would the child have Harald's wide
forehead or her thick eyelashes? Would he grow up to be
a man who didn't care if he broke the hearts of the women
who fell in love with him? Or a woman who would foolishly
entrust her heart and soul to men? I hope it's a boy, she
thought, and then soaped her white breasts. They would
swell and hurt, just like her mother had always warned
her. Breastfeeding her four daughters had inflicted cracks
on her nipples and a bulge on one of her breasts, which
had never returned to its normal dimensions. Neither had
the rest of her body. For Lupe, her mother had always been
a voluminous woman from whose chest powerful songs
emerged. Mamá couldn't pursue her singing career, but I

can. I'll do it my way, she thought, overwhelmed by what a baby would mean, not only in terms of disrupting her body but also in his need for attention, all the time she'd have to devote to him.

And who's going to work to support him?, she wondered, rubbing a natural sea sponge across her calves and feet. Weariness overcame her as if she had climbed a hundred mountains. She knew how to work hard. When her father died and they couldn't pay for her schooling at the San Antonio school anymore, she and her sister Josefina had to return to the capital. She would have much preferred to be with the nuns than living at the Hotel Principal downtown and walking to the corner of Madero and Bolívar to wait on whoever ordered the custom-made shirts that Señor Luna made. But the city was interesting and earning fifty pesos a week provided a little relief for the family. That's where the world opened up to her. It was as if money were flowing out of her hands, as if it grew there, and then she felt sure that she would never die of either hunger or boredom. That's why she went to the shows at the Principal Theater, which was on the same street as the hotel. That's what earning money was for, not to mention getting something nice to eat and paying for dance classes. Being pretty and funny was worth money, too. And if she had stayed with the nuns to get her fine education? Would she have met a nice, rich husband then? She hoped the baby wasn't a girl, or, even worse, a girl with a good figure and talent. She hoped it would be a man, clever and handsome, who knew how to offer companionship and peace to his woman. She didn't mind being a soprano at that age and she was thrilled when they chose her for the show *Rataplán* at the Lyric. All the other girls were jealous of her. And even though they had to falsify her birth certificate to send her across the border to work, she was excited when she got to L.A. at only sixteen. Back then, she didn't feel this tension in her muscles, this loneliness of living in a dream house without a family to put in it.

Lupe lifted her feet out of the bubbles and examined the red polish on her toenails. She'd have to retouch them for the evening. The party felt like an uphill battle. What if she just never got out of the bathtub? What if she just fell asleep in the warm water and perfumed soap? What if she just forgot all about Harald and the pregnancy? Would Harald come to the party? Or was he capable of giving her the excuse that he had to have dinner with his wife and children? That he just couldn't get away to come to the mansion on Rodeo Drive that belonged to Lupe, the girl from Mexico, funny Lupe, the Latin Girl, the Spitfire? She no longer had the pep that had propelled her as a young girl when Aurelio used to visit them at home and, with her sister and mamá Josefina making punch for everyone, she gave in to their special requests: Imitate María Conesa!

Dance like Celia Montalbán! Then she would ask for her sister's lipstick, paint a beauty mark on her cheek with her mother's eyeliner, and dance and sing until everyone was rolling on the floor with laughter. Then came the praise and the congratulations: Send her to dance classes, doña Josefina, this girl could go far. Aurelio Campos came knocking on their door one day, all excited, carrying his violin in its case, and saying, please, could the girl Lupe go with him? Because he had heard they were hiring girls for the new show at the Regis. Since he was a member of the orchestra, the Villalobos family trusted him, and Lupe got her little bag and hurried away with him to that audition where, when the producers saw her imitations and her style of singing and dancing, they overlooked that she was so short and so young and they hired her on the spot. Yes, she was very young back then, thought Lupe. And amputating her last name, Villalobos, didn't ensure a life free of dangers or perils of the heart, the hardest ones of all to manage.

Now they were knocking on the bathroom door and Rosita's daughter was telling her that Max was waiting to take her to get the flowers. That blessed girl, who pulled her out of her thoughts and hurried her off to get dressed quickly in tight slacks, a sweater and a green jacket, flats, and the beret that covered the hair that had not yet received the hairdresser's ministrations. Why hadn't it occurred to her to invite Aurelio? After all, he was her mentor, her godfather in this career that had allowed her to have a closet full of clothes. She would ask Edelmira to find him, and tell her to ask doña Josefina how to get in touch with him.

Roses and Tuberoses

Max started up the car and Rosita's daughter watched it pull out of the driveway as if she were looking at a Greek god leaving Paradise forever.

We'll be back soon, Lupe called to her from the car window as the girl stood there, dazed.

When was the last time someone had taken her breath away like that?

We're going to the market, Max. I want lots of tuberoses and chrysanthemums.

You're not going to buy those flowers for the dead this time? said Max jokingly, looking at her in the rearview mirror of the Lincoln.

Lupe always made an altar at home and had dinner with friends on El Día de los Muertos, the Day of the Dead. But this past November the date had caught her unprepared because she was busy trying to get back together with Harald. So, she failed to honor the tradition that made her home a meeting place for Mexican laborers and others who were undocumented here in the land of dreams, those who were responsible for making her garden look fabulous and her food the envy of all. When she gave Max the job of going to get those golden cempasúchil flowers and wrote the word down for him, she couldn't go along: She had an appointment with the doctor and didn't want anyone to know. She asked him to drop her off at the medical office and then sent him to get flowers for the dead.

No, Max, we're honoring La Virgencita de Guadalupe today. You wouldn't understand because in this country you have neither saints nor virgins. Lo siento mucho, sorry. But today's my saint's day.

Max glanced at her again in the mirror. He liked his boss's sense of humor and the way she called him handsome and treated him warmly, like a friend. It also gave him a real kick that his friends teased him about being the Mexican woman's lover and that his wife was jealous.

Querida, I know all her lovers: they're big fish, not regular guys like me.

He said that because of Gary Cooper, Johnny Weissmuller, and Arturo de Córdova, to name a few. But his wife stopped believing him when they started publishing photos of Lupe Vélez with Harald Ramond, who was just an extra. Then she went on the attack: That guy's an extra, just like you, Max. It cut him to the core. On the one hand, he wasn't proud of his boss's new relationship. On the other hand, he wasn't an extra: he was a supporting actor in the domestic life of la Señora Lupe.

Are you feeling okay? Max asked when he saw Lupe's gloomy face.

I must adorn myself, my dear Max. I require my makeup artist.

But Max knew that wasn't the problem. He'd seen her many times without makeup and Lupe's glowing skin and shining eyes were always extraordinary. He drove her to Paramount Studios and back. He knew what she was like with her hair as glossy as a wet otter, bags under her eyes from overwork, woozy from alcohol after a dinner party, aggressive and brittle during the divorce from Mr. Weissmuller. He held out his hand to help her out of the car and walked with her among the flower stalls.

You choose, Max. You know what I like.

He knew that defeated tone of voice. A few months ago, he had brought her back home from the studio where Señor de Córdova was shooting a picture. Something had happened in the Mexican actor's trailer because it took her a while to come out, and when she did, she was alone. He didn't dare ask if Señor de Córdova would be catching up with them, and then Lupe told him to start the car. When they got to Rodeo Drive, she asked him inside to have a drink with her. Max poured two vodkas and sat down next to the woman on one of the rocks out in the garden. The sky was clear, and Lupe clinked her glass against his.

Max, you're a married man. Do you understand why a man makes a woman fall in love with him when he knows he can't dedicate his life to her?

It's not every day a fellow meets a woman as charming and beautiful as you.

That's what I say, said Lupe, taking a sip.

Max searched for the right words to cheer up his boss. He knew he was witnessing her breakup with Señor Arturo.

They're idiots.

This time, it was him who clinked the glass against hers. He was married to a nice, quiet woman who was a good mother and kept the house in order. A decent and boring life, he thought, and he didn't know what he'd do if he weren't able to participate in a noisy, festive life like Señora Lupe's. But he didn't want any trouble. He had lived through that when his mother ran off with a friend of the family. He knew that infidelity created an irreparable hole inside that stifled anyone who fell victim to it. He didn't plan to make his children and wife suffer that way, no matter how many Katies and Lindas he ran into. A kiss maybe, a look, a dance at the Dusk Club maybe, but that was all.

Why do you always go out with married men? he said, emboldened by the vodka.

Is there any other kind, Max?

Max chose bunches of tuberoses, bouquets of white chrysanthemums, and some pink carnations while Lupe followed him around, floating amid the petals' freshness and perfume, but paying little attention to this task that she usually enjoyed.

We need roses, Max.

She never bought roses. Her lovers were the ones who gave her those luxurious, thorny bouquets. But he didn't want to contradict her.

Are the red ones okay?

No. Yellow. Lots of them.

When they got back to the house, Rosita's daughter and Edelmira hurried out to help. Edelmira had a message for her: Mister John had called and said he couldn't come to the party. Lupe didn't seem to hear.

Max, tear off all those rose petals and throw them into the pool. And then leave me alone, all of you.

Lupe watched the yellow petals floating on the sunny surface of the water. She looked around to make sure they had done as she had asked. Then she took off her shoes, sweater, pants, and, wearing only the champagne-colored lingerie that Arturo or Gary — no, it had been Johnny — had given her, she let herself fall in among the flowers, which parted for the unexpected mermaid. The cool water calmed her as the petals clung to her arms and wet hair.

Yes, the lingerie was from Johnny, her Tarzan, that sweet
Romanian she had married, the only one who had shared
her bed legally—and who had left it the exact same way.

The King of the Jungle

It started during the theater season in New York City, when
she appeared with Cole Porter on Broadway in *You Never
Know*. It's true, you never know, she said later when she
signed the marriage book as Guadalupe Villalobos Vélez
next to Weissmuller's signature. She had used her legal,
given name and Johnny laughed: Yours is as long as mine!

But yours wasn't the name of a general, boasted Lupe,
whose father Jacobo had fought in the Mexican Revolution.

She liked New York City, although being Latina—as they
called her—didn't make her as unique there as it did in
Hollywood. Here, the Puerto Rican girls danced and sang,
too, but the difference was that Lupe's English was as good
as her Spanish and she could exaggerate her south of the
border accent or hide it at will. The nuns at the San Antonio
school had started the good work that her years in Los
Angeles had finished. But there was no time to sit around at
home twiddling her thumbs: her career was in decline, and
she was still running into prejudice.

She needed to breathe some new air and it was an honor
to tie her star to a musician as important as Cole Porter. She

lived at the Plaza Hotel, between Fifth and Sixth Avenues at Central Park South, and she felt as if she were in one of those movies that she'd seen but never acted in. She liked how the women dressed, the elegance of the men. She could walk everywhere, forget about her Lincoln Continental, Max, and the need to rely on someone all the time to take her to work and bring her home. New York felt a little bit like Mexico City: the streets, the taxis, eating in cafés, the hotdog vendors on the corners, the sold-out theater and her face on the playbill outside, the applause. The movies didn't give her that direct feedback. Here, there were eyes, laughter, whispers, and bouquets of flowers at the end of the show. Onstage, Lupe Vélez was a flesh and blood actress.

That's what she thought when she saw Johnny in the hotel elevator, too: wide-backed, strong, square-jawed, big hands, tall. He was flesh and blood and she wanted to gnaw on him. She called his room:

I'm on the floor above yours and I'm waiting for you here. This is Lupe Vélez.

Only for the big guy to make fun of her! She didn't know whether he was mocking her English or of her desire to see him. But no one got away with hanging up on her! She called back to insult him in Spanish:

Who do you think you are, you smug bastard? Better men than you have been in my bed! I'm not starving! Get lost, you son of a bitch.

In a few minutes, the big man was knocking at her door looking like a sweet little puppy. He apologized, saying that he thought someone was playing a trick on him until he found out that Lupe Vélez was actually staying there at the hotel.

I went to the premiere of your movie, *Tarzan*.

A bottle awaited from which Lupe poured herself a drink, but Johnny didn't drink and instead joined her with a seltzer on the rocks while he allowed Lupe to slowly seduce him with her flattery and sassiness, to strip him naked as if he were her personal property, and finally, a few days later, he declared his intention to marry that little Mexican spitfire. Not long after, the big man and the little lady signed a marriage license in Nevada, had a ball in L.A., and made love in London, where Johnny was working and got his first surprise. What a jealous drama Lupe acted out for him! How was Lupe supposed to believe that her big lump of meat wasn't going to strike the fancy of every young (and even not so young) woman who crossed his path? They had seen him in a loincloth, they imagined what his caresses would be like, his power to swim into a woman's body, submerge himself inside her, and liquefy her until he made her explode in an Olympic performance. As a lover, Johnny continued to be a swimmer with impeccable form, precision, endurance, and velocity as needed. Lupe's jealousy was proportional to his lovemaking skill. Johnny and the water, Johnny and the two dogs, Mr. Kelly and Mrs. Murphy.

The problems started as soon as he moved in with her: according to him, her chihuahuas were annoying as well as ugly, and the parakeet was an affront to the marriage because it kept desperately screeching, *Gary!* What personal space did he have in the mansion, aside from the pool? That's why he showed up one day with his very own dog, Otto. It was too hard for him to live in Lupe's house with Lupe's servants, decorations, parties, music, and Lupe's food. Her sense of humor saved the day, though. She always knew how to make him laugh, but then later she infuriated him again. Lupe knew that she was able to get both the best out of that swimmer-turned-movie-star, and the worst: his rage. If only Johnny had matched her drink for drink instead of acting like such a stiff, so utterly uncomprehending of his Mexican girl when she didn't feel like sailing in the *Allure* while he raced his pals to Catalina Island. She felt utterly lost in that trio of handsome navigators: Humphrey Bogart in his *Santana* and Errol Flynn in his *Sirocco*.

Lupe stepped out of the water with rose petals stuck to her skin, put her clothes on over her wet body, and went inside. Mrs. Murphy and Mr. Kelly, her poor chihuahuas, had died by then, and all her old companions were long gone. Ever since Johnny wrung the parakeet's neck, she didn't want pets anymore.

Yes, said Lupe out of pure spite when she came home from a shoot, I poisoned Otto.

And Johnny, beside himself, took hold of the insolent bird who endlessly cried *Gary*! and held it by the neck until it expired in his huge hands. Lupe screamed. He had crossed the line. Their life of constant fighting had proved impossible. But she had still wanted Johnny to come to her party. It didn't matter to her anymore if he came with the quiet woman he had chosen, that rich little homebody, Beryl Scott. But he left a message that he couldn't come: you know, the filming and blah-blah-blah. After the divorce, she only saw him once more, eating with Ed Sullivan at Toots Shor's.

So you're getting married again? she overheard Ed say to Johnny.

Back to hell, he answered. I've already been there.

But it wasn't true. For Lupe, hell had begun only recently, when she first set her eyes on one of the extras in Arturo's film at the time: the perky Austrian, Harald Ramond.

It was one thing for Lupe to live as she pleased in her Beverly Hills house and to get work in Hollywood with the so-called Spanish style that Gary liked so much when they were first introduced. It was quite another to want to be cast in a Mexican film. So, when Fernando de Fuentes called her to film *La Zandunga*, she didn't think twice: she said yes. Goodbye to face-offs with Tarzan and hello to a chance to spend time with her mother and sisters. A rest from all that English with the exaggerated Spanish accent, goodbye to the little cordovan hats and polka dot skirts that made her look Hispanic, a Latina, but not what she was: a Mexican woman. She wasn't mistaken when she made the decision that would take her to live in her own country for a few months, first in the capital and then in Oaxaca. She was sure she'd made the right choice when they placed the resplandor on her, the headpiece that was the traditional costume of the women of the Isthmus de Tehuantepec, which covered her hair and put her features on display, emphasizing her face by framing it with a white, lace frill. It wasn't for nothing it was called a resplandor—a radiance—because it looked like rays of light. It wasn't a mistake to take that job, which, even though it didn't pay as much in dollars, afforded her the comfort of her native castellano and praise for her looks, those enormous, dark eyes with their curtain of thick eyelashes and those classic high cheekbones. It wasn't a mistake, either, when Señor de Fuentes introduced the stars at that meeting and she met Arturo de Córdova, the man with whom she would share top billing.

I can't resist, she said that night while munching on tamales back at her mother's house.

Aprovecha, daughter, eat as many as you want. Doña Josefina thought she was referring to the dish she liked so much and didn't get to eat often at her American mansion.

She's not talking about the food, mamá, said Mercedes, who had accompanied her sister to Estudios Churubusco.

He's so handsome, so attentive, so Mexican! Lupe said defensively.

Señor Arturo de Córdova, mamá. He's in the movie, her sister explained.

Lupe took a bite of a green tamale and her eyes shone with pleasure. And so delicious! The tamal, I mean.

The sisters giggled, but doña Josefina's face grew serious. My girl, you've already given them enough to gossip about with you and Johnny.

Oh, don't be so serious, mamá. I'm here to spend time with you.

And with Señor de Córdova, said Mercedes softly.

Lupe was in high spirits. She had forgotten what it felt like to be in the bosom of her family. Some time ago, Mercedes and her mother had visited her and stayed for almost a month at the house. She enjoyed having them there, no matter how much the mistress of the mansion she had to be, or how frequently she had to come and go for work. But that time, filming in Mexico, being with her people, felt like just the vacation she needed. Maybe that's why Arturo attracted her so much, because he had the demeanor that suited her, for a change.

You lucky little thing, the costume designer said.

And it was true. Thanks to being just short of five feet

tall, her destiny was to always look up, like the song said. Arturo was in the category of handsome leading man and, as such, he was married.

Lucky? How? she said to Manlio as he arranged her skirt and stuck pins in it to adjust the waistband. He's already taken.

Well, from what I see, there's plenty to go around, he said.

It wasn't only Manlio who noticed Arturo's gazes aimed at the chaparrita and his solicitousness to her after a day of filming. In the trailers and backstage, the rumors went wild about Lupe Vélez's new romance, and Lupe let herself be loved. Why not? After all, she was going to go back to the United States, so the affair could only last while they filmed *La Zandunga*. It wasn't as if she didn't have experience saying goodbye and being with married men. It's just that she hadn't ever tried out the Mexican national product, that forwardness, the kind of treatment women received, the style of flattery, the jokes. Because everyone laughs best in their own language, and compliments are caresses in Spanish.

How delicious you are, chaparrita. You sweet little shortie, you tiny bit of heaven, my queen, my chula, my lovely.

She liked how Arturo said chula, especially when he came up from behind her and whispered in a naughty tone of voice: You look rechula, so gorgeous, will you allow me to pay you a visit tonight?

Lupe and Arturo rented a room at the Hotel Palacio and she explained to her family that the production company offered that amenity so that she could rest during the long, hard shooting schedule. But rest was the last thing she wanted, and she relished the Yucatecan's audacity in loving her. She liked how he bathed her in the tub as if she were a little girl. Arturo looked at her body hungrily: he couldn't believe how perfectly-proportioned the short little woman was.

Who would believe that one day I would meet Lupe Vélez?

Don't be a sycophant, Lupe snapped, lolling in bed after their lovemaking.

I saw you with Laurel and Hardy and you were so funny. I love how you made me laugh, how you weren't the typical femme fatale.

Well, allow me to disappoint you: I am a femme fatale.

I don't care about your lovers from the past.

But I do, quipped Lupe.

I know that Gary was even the name of your parakeet.

Don't remind me.

Will you call the next one Arturito?

And what if someone wrings his neck?

Arturo began to move slowly up her legs, biting them

softly. Lupe was swooning happily into her pillow. They cavorted some more and ended up exhausted, their bodies tangled in sleep until Arturo realized how late it was and jumped up to dress and go home. Lupe was so tired, she barely opened her eyes. The next day she reproached him on the set:

You don't just leave me like that as if I were a prostitute. You're mine, period.

And so, the affair dried up for a spell. Lupe would go to sleep at her mother's house, and she refused the flowers that Señor de Córdova sent her, despite all the cries from doña Josefina of good heavens, daughter, look how pretty they are! It wasn't enough, and Lupe understood that, once again, her life had gotten messy. But every time they made up, it was better than the time before: They enjoyed each other more, they had more fun, and they fell deeper in love. When the filming was over, even though Lupe tried to stay on for as long as possible, Arturo couldn't find any good excuses for spending as much time with her. They made a last date in the Hotel Palacio and then they checked out. Lupe insisted that it had to happen that way, and that she was going directly back home. She couldn't stand being in Mexico without meeting up with Arturo at all hours. It wasn't enough for her anymore to just be among family: She wanted to be in that man's arms.

Come with me, Lupe said.

Find me some work.

If I do, you have to stay with me.

And a little while later, Lupe made it happen. Arturo was called to an audition to play in *For Whom the Bell Tolls*. He didn't understand that she wasn't just talking about his stay during the shoot, but rather about staying for a life together. And even though it was clear to him that he would be sharing the credits with none other than Gary Cooper, his ambition and desire to see his girlfriend overcame his discomfort that two of Lupe's lovers would be together in the same movie. It wasn't just any movie, either: it was based on the novel by Ernest Hemingway, one of the most popular and respected writers of the moment. He had read the book himself. And the proximity to Gary wasn't just on the set, because he lived near Lupe, too. Occasionally, Arturo got jealous, to the delight of the Mexican women, who already wanted him to move in with her.

Stay in Hollywood, she said to him while they had drinks at the pool on those June nights. You know things will go your way. There's no lack of work, and the Red Scare is dying down.

It's easier for you to go back to Mexico to star in a movie, he said.

Lupe had returned to Mexico City several times, accepting invitations or on the pretext of visiting her family.

It's not so easy to get to film a movie with Gary at MGM.

They won't let go of you so easily, she said.

Them? Or you?

Arturo was right, thought Lupe, gazing at the slow summer sunset: It was she who didn't want to let him leave. She was already thirty-three and by this point she wanted a man to stay with her for keeps.

I already delivered on my promise to find you something here. I need you to come through on your promise, too.

Affectionately, Lupe lifted his feet onto her lap.

You speak Spanish, you're an actor, loving, handsome. Why would I want to let you go?

Don't let me go, begged Arturo as Lupe dragged him off to her bedroom.

But those were just words, the same over-the-top words others had said before. A few days later, even though she warned him that if he left, he would never again set foot in her house, Arturo went out to the carport with his suitcase. Lupe screamed at Max from the window that he had better not even consider giving him a lift to the airport, but she ended up sitting inside the car, leaning against the chest of that kind man, feeling like she was losing a piece of herself.

Why won't you stay? she kept asking tenderly at the airport.

You know the reasons, Lupita.

Don't Lupita me. Just plain Lupe.

There's nothing I would like more.

What parakeet drool. Hey, why don't you go tell that witch of a wife to get you a role in a feature film. . .

It was 1943, almost four years of coming and going, but this time Lupe's anger stood in the way of a loving goodbye kiss, a playful pinch, or Arturo's *take good care of them for me* as he gazed at the actress's shapely legs. When she got into the car with Max to return home, she changed the plan:

Take me to Long Beach. I need to see the ocean.

The Extra

Edelmira had taken care of ironing her dress. The grape-colored shoes were impeccable. The stylist finished Lupe's hair and, as she left the bedroom, the actress asked her to send Max up. It was time to get dressed. The first guests were starting to arrive. The waiters were under the direction of her housekeeper, the music was being taken care of by Edel. Max knocked at her door and Lupe, retouching her eyelashes in the mirror, told him to come in.

Max, I want the carnations in my room.

All of them? he asked, intrigued.

Set them around in lots of vases. I don't want to sleep without the company of something beautiful.

As Max was leaving, she called out to him:

And votive candles. . . for my virgencita.

The party began to get underway when the band played *Stella by Starlight*. Martinis, bourbon, and beers were being served. The light from the garden beckoned the guests to look out at the greenery, but the chill of the evening kept everyone inside. Ramón Navarro, Lili Damita, Gilbert Roland, and Estelle Taylor were in attendance. But Gary, even though he was her neighbor, didn't show. Johnny had sent his regrets. Evasively, Arturo said he would try to come, although Lupe's recent relationship with Harald made him uncomfortable. And Harald, just as Lupe had suspected since she woke up on that December 13th, wouldn't come or even make an excuse, send a gift, or offer a single kind gesture to the woman who was carrying his child. He didn't want any complications, that much was crystal clear. Neither did he want another child, Lupe saw that now. He wanted to have a good time. Somebody had already warned her: He's a freeloader, watch your pocketbook. While she was drinking her third martini and watching Edel dance with one of the guests, she thought about how the one thing she never took care of was her own heart, that tattered organ that was now beating in synch with that of the baby she was carrying inside her small, much-desired, much-caressed, much-used body. She was so tired. She felt light-headed. *Cry me a river*. Why don't they play something cheerful? A little Mexican tune. She had sung already, and for some reason these sad melodies, the darkest ones, made everyone forget all about Lupe. That's how she was able to slip away by herself into the garden and gaze up at the stars. She said adiós to them. As she went upstairs, she said adiós to the music, too, which grew fainter and fainter at her back. When she closed her bedroom door, she left everyone she knew and loved outside. As she took off her grape-colored shoes at the edge of the bed, she contemplated the feet that had taken her here and there, and she thought that it was only right to let them rest now. When she opened the bottle of Seconal and swallowed one pill after another, she remembered that she had forgotten something: the words that explained why she was leaving. They would be a kindness to her mother. She was still lucid enough to denounce Harald for refusing to be a father to their child, for refusing to love her. Then, although she no longer had the strength to write it down, she thought that he was like an extra in her life, a redundant person. What an irony that she should be carrying his baby and that the truly superfluous one should be an innocent child.

One by one, she lit the votive candles to the Virgin of Guadalupe, made the sign of the cross, and looked at herself in the mirror one last time. She didn't want to look poorly, even in death. She felt a wave of dizziness and was about to faint, but she made it to the bed in time to lie down, surrounded by carnations and the flickering light that slowly died down. Then she heard her own girlish laughter and she saw herself with her sisters, imitating María Conesa.

Bravo, Lupe, bravo.

SANTIAGO ACOSTA is an Assistant Professor in the Department of Spanish and Portuguese at Yale University and an award-winning poet. His fourth and most recent collection, *El próximo desierto*, earned him the José Emilio Pacheco Literature Prize "Ciudad y Naturaleza." In 2024, Spain's Visor Libros released a collection of his selected poetry, titled *La desesperanza*. He has received support from the DAAD Artists-in-Berlin Program and was an invited poet at the United Nations Climate Change Conference COP26 in Glasgow. While in Caracas, he co-founded the poetry journal *El Salmón*, which won a National Book Award in 2010.

MANUEL ARDUINO PAVÓN was born in Montevideo in 1955 and currently lives in Buenos Aires. A prolific writer, keenly interested in experimental forms of writing and both Western and Eastern theosophy and esotericism, Pavón's most famous works are the surreal pamphlet *200 palestinas para un músculo* (1975) and the book of microfiction *El libro de las ruinas azules: historias arquetípicas y maravillosas* (1991).

ELVIRA BLANCO is a Venezuelan researcher, translator, and PhD candidate in the Department of Latin American and Iberian Cultures at Columbia University. She has worked as an editor for academic and non-academic publications in Spanish and English.

JENNY BURTON is a literary translator and urban planner based in Boston, Massachusetts. Her translation work focuses on contemporary poetry and first-person narratives from Latin America.

ANSILTA GRIZAS is an Argentine writer. She has published two books: *Un temporal*, which was released in both Argentina (Editorial Entropía, 2021) and Chile (Editorial Bastante, 2022), and *Río de lava* (Cumulus Nimbus, 2022). She lives and works in Buenos Aires.

RAMÓN HONDAL is a Cuban poet who lives in Havana. Hondal is the author of *Diálogos* (Ediciones Extramuros, 2014), *Scratch* (Bokeh Press, 2018), and *Prótesis* (Casa Vacía, 2019). In 2013, Hondal received the Luis Rogelio Nogueras Award for *Diálogos*. Hondal belongs to the so-called "Generación Cero" of Cuban writers, who came of age during the Special Period and began to publish their work in the early 2000s. Hondal serves as an editor for poet Reina María Rodríguez's Torre de Letras imprint.

ELENA LAHR-VIVAZ is a writer, translator, and professor. Lahr-Vivaz received her PhD in Hispanic Studies from the University of Pennsylvania, and holds the post of Associate Professor of Spanish at Rutgers University–Newark, where she specializes in Latin American literature and film. She is the author of *Writing Islands: Space and Identity in the Transnational Cuban Archipelago* (University of Florida Press, 2022); and *Mexican Melodrama: Film and Nation from the Golden Age to the New Wave* (University of Arizona Press, 2016).

MÓNICA LAVÍN is a Mexican author of six books of short stories, notable among them *Ruby Tuesday no ha muerto* (1996 recipient of the Gilberto Owen National Literary Prize); *Uno no sabe* (2003, finalist for the Antonin Artaud award); and her most recent collection, *La corredora de Cuemanco y el aficionado a Schubert* (2008). She was awarded the Elena Poniatowska Ibero-American Novel Prize for *Yo, la peor* (2010), and *Cuando te hablen de amor* (2017) was a finalist for the 2019 Mario Vargas Llosa Biennial Prize for the Novel. She is currently a professor in the Creative Writing Department of the Universidad Autónoma de la Ciudad de México in México City.

SARA LISSA PAULSON learned Spanish in the streets of Sevilla with Antonio Marín Márquez, his bandmates, friends, and family. It was there that she got her first translation job at age 19 for a local music zine. She holds degrees in Comparative Literature, Spanish, Bilingual Education, and Library Science. She has worked as a children's librarian in NYC's alternative elementary and high schools for over 21 years, reading aloud day in and day out, and teaches future librarians of all ages at Queens College's Graduate School of Library and Information Studies.

MERCEDES ROFFÉ is one of Argentina's leading poets. Widely published in Latin America and Spain, her poetry has also been published in translation in Italy, Quebec, Romania, England, and the United States. In 1998 she founded Pen Press, Plaquettes de Poesía, a successful tiny press dedicated to the publication of contemporary Spanish-language poets as well as poets of other languages in Spanish translation. Among other distinctions, she was awarded a John Simon Guggenheim Fellowship in poetry (2001). She has published *Poemas* (1978), *El tapiz de Ferdinand Oziel* (1983), *Cámara baja* (1987), *La noche y las palabras* (1996), *Definiciones Mayas* (2000), *Antología poética* (2000), *Canto errante* (2002), *Memorial de agravios* (2002), and *La ópera fantasma* (2006), and *Las linternas flotantes* (2009).

LUCINA SCHELL is the International Rights Manager at the University of Chicago Press, and a member of the Third Coast Translators Collective. She translates primarily poetry from Spanish. Published translations include Daiana Henderson's *So That Something Remains Lit* (2018) and *Vision of the Children of Evil* by Miguel Ángel Bustos (2018), as well as selections from authors including Erika Martínez, Graciela Cros, Ada Salas, and María Ángeles Pérez López.

D. P. SNYDER is a bilingual writer and translator from Spanish. Her book-length translations include *Scary Story* by Alberto Chimal (2023), *Arrhythmias* by Angelina Muñiz-Huberman (2022), *Meaty Pleasures* by Mónica Lavín (2021), and *33 Dreams* by Juan Carlos Garvayo (019). Her work has been published in *Ploughshares*, *Two Lines*, *Exile Quarterly*, *The Southern Review*, *The Georgia Review*, *Latin American Literature Today*, *World Literature Today*, and elsewhere. Her translation of Mónica Lavín's "Coyoacán a la carte" (WLT, Nov. 2022) was nominated for a Pushcart Prize.

TIFFANY TROY is a critic, translator, and poet. She is the author of the chapbook *When Ilium Burns*, as well as co-translator of Santiago Acosta's *The Coming Desert*, in collaboration with the 4W International Women Collective Translation Project at the University of Wisconsin-Madison. Her literary criticism, translation, and creative writing are published in *The Adroit Journal*, *BOMB Magazine*, *The Cortland Review*, *EcoTheo Review*, *Hong Kong Review of Books*, *Latin American Literature Today*, *The Laurel Review*, *The Los Angeles Review*, *Matter*, *New World Writing*, *Rain Taxi*, and *Tupelo Quarterly*, where she is Managing Editor.

Printed in the USA
CPSIA information can be obtained
at www.ICGtesting.com
JSHW082033250624
65313JS00001B/1

9 798987 926475